An enormous monster sat on the lawn. It was as big as a car!

Shiny green scales covered its body.

There were little horns on its forehead, and nubby wings behind each shoulder.

Hank watched the thing skulk across the yard. A large silver serving spoon hung from its slobbery mouth like a toothpick.

"What the...?"

And then Hank saw something else. Something that took his breath away. The chain he had tied around Montana last night was dangling from the monster's neck.

"Montana!" Hank gasped.

To my devoted dog, Montana.
—P. H.

For my family—who are the
source of magic in my life.
—N. E.

Text copyright © 1997 by Nate Evans and Paul Hindman.
Illustrations copyright © 1997 by Nate Evans.
Cover illustration copyright © 1997 by Jeff Spackman.

http://www.randomhouse.com/

Library of Congress Cataloging-in-Publication Data
Hindman, Paul.
Dragon bones / by Paul Hindman and Nate Evans.
p. cm. "A Stepping stone book."
SUMMARY: Hank is worried that he and his mother will have to move from Boulder, but he has even bigger problems when a wizard trapped in a tree in his backyard asks Hank to help him destroy the evil dragon that Hank's dog has unleashed.
ISBN 0-679-87435-6 (trade). — ISBN 0-679-97435-0 (lib. bdg.)
[1. Magic—Fiction. 2. Wizards—Fiction. 3. Dragons—Fiction.]
I. Evans, Nate, ill. II. Title.
PZ7.H56965Dr 1997
[Fic]—dc21 96-37482

Printed in the United States of America 10 9 8 7 6 5 4 3 2 1

DRAGON BONES

by Paul Hindman and Nate Evans

illustrated by Nate Evans

A STEPPING STONE BOOK

Random House New York

1

Hank huddled in the dark hall, listening to his mother. She was talking on the kitchen phone.

Hank had never eavesdropped before. But tonight he had to listen. He had just heard her say, "I don't think we're going to make it."

Didn't think they were going to make it? What was she talking about? His heart almost stopped. Of course he had to hear more.

"Boulder's too expensive," she said. "I know, Peg. You told me. But I thought this job would pay enough. We had to go *some*where. After Pete died..." She didn't go on.

5

That always happened, Hank noticed. Whenever she mentioned his father, she choked up. Couldn't go on.

Hank's dad had died seven months ago. And his mother still couldn't talk about it. Hank was trying to be the man of the house now. But he was only nine years old.

They had just moved to Boulder, Colorado. He loved it there. He had made lots of friends. There was always something to do. Everyone had a mountain bike. They all went camping just about every weekend.

And now she wanted to leave?

"Hank's happy here," his mother went on. "And I really like working at the mall. But we can't stay. I can barely pay the rent!"

Hank felt something wet on his ear. "Yuck!" he blurted out.

Montana, his big black Labrador retriever, tried to lick him again. Hank pushed him away.

"Honey?" his mother called. "Is that you?"

"Uh, yeah!" Hank answered sheepishly. "Just going to the bathroom. 'Night, Mom!

"Thanks, mutt," he grumbled as they shuffled off to his room. "Now I'll never know what Mom's gonna do, until she does it.

"We got trouble," he continued. "Money trouble. We either gotta move, or you gotta cut down on bones."

Montana whimpered.

"Lighten up," the boy said. "It was just a joke."

Hank turned his light off and slipped into bed. Montana climbed up and laid his head on Hank's chest. "I gotta do something to help Mom," Hank muttered. He drifted off to sleep, thinking of ways to earn money. Lots of it. And fast.

2

The next day after school, Hank sat in the kitchen.

At the top of a blank page, he wrote MONEY-MAKING SCHEMES. He liked that word. "Schemes." It made him feel grown-up. Under that, he scribbled:

Paper Route
Mow Lawns
Car Washing
Dog Washing

After that, he was stumped. He nibbled the eraser. Through the window, he watched

Montana in the backyard. The dog seemed to be interested in something. Something large, poking out of the ground.

Hank dropped his pencil and went out back.

Montana pawed the earth. He was digging at something in a hole. He chomped at the thing, then dug some more. Hank moved closer. Montana growled at him.

"Hey, mutt. It's okay!"

Then Hank saw it.

It was a bone. A huge bone.

"It's gotta be a...a *dinosaur* bone!" he gasped.

He ran to the garage and grabbed a shovel.

"Here, dog," he said, "let me get that monster bone outta there."

Montana snarled.

"Hey, Montana!" Hank scolded. "Watch your manners!"

He started digging. Montana clamped his teeth onto the shovel handle and growled.

Hank stared at the dog. "What's the matter?" he asked. He grabbed Montana's collar. "Come on. Inside."

He dragged the big black dog toward the house. Montana struggled and squirmed the whole way. He even nipped at Hank's hand. Weird. Not typical Montana behavior at all.

Hank managed to shove the struggling dog into the kitchen. "Bad dog! Stay!" He slammed the door.

Hank went back and dug for a long time.

As he dug, he kept hearing the dog in the house, barking and growling. Every once in a while, Hank saw Montana jump up at the window, clawing at the glass.

Finally, Hank uncovered the entire bone.

It was enormous. Maybe it was the rib of a triceratops! Or a *Tyrannosaurus rex!*

He threw the shovel down and rushed inside. He looked up a number in the phone book. Hands shaking, he dialed it.

Montana stood beside him, watching.

"Denver Museum of Natural History," a man's voice answered.

"I just found a dinosaur bone!" Hank blurted out.

"Is this a prank?" the voice said.

"No! I really found a dinosaur bone in my backyard. A *huge* one!"

"That's highly unlikely," the voice said.

"But if it *is* a dinosaur bone, would you buy it?"

"Well…" the voice hesitated. "The museum will certainly want to investigate."

"And *buy* it?" Hank pressed.

"If it *is* a dinosaur bone, then yes," the man replied.

"Thanks! I'll call you back real soon!"

Hank hung up and whooped.

Saved by a bone!

With the money the museum gave him, he'd be able to help his mom pay the rent. They'd be able to stay in Boulder. Maybe there'd be money left over to buy a bunch of cool stuff. Skis and a mountain bike, maybe even a new car for his mom and...

Montana was outside again.

And he had the bone!

"Oh, no!" Hank yelled. The dog was gnawing the bone to splinters!

Hank tore outside. "What've you done? You've totally trashed it!"

Montana stopped gnawing and looked up at the boy. He bared his teeth in a snarl.

"Whoa. Back off!" Hank said.

The dog went back to chewing.

Slobber dripped on his paws.

Something was wrong.

Then Montana lifted a heavy chunk of bone and dragged it off into the bushes.

He was moving oddly. Slinking off. Crawling on his belly. Not like a dog. More like a lizard. Like a big black lizard.

Hank shivered and went back to the house.

So much for the bone, the money, and his dreams.

Then he heard his dog howling. It wasn't a sound a dog would make. It was louder and much, much deeper. Not a doggy sound. *Not at all!*

3

"Montana! Montana!"

Hank called as he rode his bike down one street after another. But Montana wasn't anywhere. And Hank had looked just about everywhere.

He finally gave up and rode home. His mom was just pulling into the driveway.

"Mom!" Hank wailed. "Montana's gone! I've looked everywhere!"

"Hop in," his mom suggested, "and we'll take another look."

They looked until dark. No dog.

"He's around somewhere, Hank," his mom assured him as they pulled into the garage. "You'll see. He'll come back."

But Hank was still worried when he got ready for bed. It didn't seem the same without Montana.

He was tossing his dirty clothes into the closet when he heard muffled breathing. He froze. Something was inside his closet! He looked in. It was dark. He heard raspy breathing.

"Montana!" Hank cried. "Where've you been?"

Montana whimpered and inched forward. "What's the matter, boy?" Hank asked.

The dog looked strange. His eyes were all red. And his jaw was swollen!

"What is it, boy? Did you cut yourself on that old monster bone? Huh?"

Hank knelt and looked inside the dog's

mouth. He gasped and fell backward.

Montana's breath smelled rotten! Like a dead skunk!

"Oh, Montana," Hank said. "Did that old bone make you sick?"

He patted the dog's head. "If you're sick, boy, I don't know what we're gonna do. We can't afford to take you to the vet."

Montana slinked to the far corner of the

room. He huddled there, shivering.

Hank's mother knocked on the bedroom door. "All ready for bed?" she called.

Hank frantically grabbed the pile of clothes from the closet and threw it over his dog. Then he quickly jumped onto the bed.

For some reason—he wasn't sure why—he didn't want his mother to see Montana like this. Maybe she'd phone the ASPCA or the police or something.

"Yeah. Come in," he said.

"Honey," his mother said as she came into the room, "please promise me you'll fill in that hole in the backyard."

"I said I would, Mom."

His mother ruffled his hair fondly. "Digging for dinosaur bones…at your age."

"Yeah. Well…"

She had been furious at first about the mess in the backyard. And, of course, Hank couldn't prove anything, since Montana had eaten the evidence!

And now he prayed she wouldn't see Montana in the corner, looking all strange.

"So, how was work today, anyway?" he asked lamely.

"Not bad."

"We don't have to leave Boulder, do we?"

Hank's mother looked at him oddly. "What do you mean?"

"I don't know. I just don't want to leave. I wish Dad was here."

"Oh, honey. So do I." Her voice caught.

Hank said, "I miss him. I wish..." He trailed off.

"What, sweetie?"

"I just wish he hadn't died. It isn't fair!"

Hank heard Montana moan. The boy faked a coughing fit. He shifted in the bed, making the springs squeak loudly.

His mother looked at him closely. "I hope you're not coming down with anything," she said.

"I'm fine," Hank said.

"Okay. Well, good night," his mom said. "I love you."

She kissed Hank on the cheek. "See you in the morning." She walked to the door.

Before she closed it, she asked, "You sure you're okay?"

"Yeah."

"Okay. And, Hank, don't worry. Montana'll be back."

"What?" Hank asked, confused. Montana *was* back. "Oh. Right."

She switched off the light and closed the door.

In the dark, Hank heard Montana snuffling in the corner.

"C'mere, boy," Hank whispered.

The dog didn't leap onto the bed. He didn't put his head on Hank's chest. He stayed over in the corner, making funny noises.

"Good night, Montana," Hank whispered. "Hope you feel better soon."

Montana lifted his head.

Hank saw two burning red eyes.

They glowed at him from the dark corner. Not like a dog's eyes at all!

More like a monster's!

4

Hank didn't sleep well that night. He kept looking over to where Montana's eyes glowed like an eerie night-light. Now the dog was drooling and whining.

Just after midnight Hank got up and chained the trembling animal to the bedpost. He used the strong chain he had gotten when Montana was a pup.

"Sorry, boy," he said, patting Montana. "This is for your own good."

Sometime before dawn, he fell asleep. He awoke with a start, the sun shining into his eyes.

"Hey, boy," he said as he tossed his blankets aside.

But Montana wasn't there!

A fragment of the chain was still wrapped around the bedpost. The rest was gone. Torn loose!

Hank jumped out of bed and ran to the door. It was open, hanging crookedly on its hinges. The knob was completely crushed.

Then he heard his mother scream!

He tore down the hall.

"We've been robbed!" his mom shouted. "All my jewelry's gone! Check the rest of the house. *We've been robbed!*"

Hank dashed to the living room. The TV was still there. So was the stereo.

"Everything's here!" he called out.

"The silverware!" his mom shrieked from the kitchen.

Hank bolted into the kitchen. It looked as

if a bomb had gone off! His mom stood staring at the wreckage. She held the empty silverware drawer.

"This is…this is…" his mom said, and dropped the drawer. "This is too much! What next? They took everything! My jewelry. The silver. Even…your dad's gold watch!"

The watch? His dad had gotten that watch when he was a young man. Hank was supposed to get it when he went to college.

"We'd better call the police," his mother said. "You get ready for school, honey. I'll take care of it."

She reached for the phone. As she dialed, Hank saw something move in the backyard.

He ran to the window.

An enormous monster sat on the lawn. It was as big as a car!

Shiny green scales covered its body.

There were little horns on its forehead,

and nubby wings behind each shoulder.

Hank watched the thing skulk across the yard. A large silver serving spoon hung from its slobbery mouth like a toothpick.

"What the...?"

And then Hank saw something else. Something that took his breath away. The chain he had tied around Montana last night was dangling from the monster's neck.

"Montana!" Hank gasped.

5

All that day at school Hank sweated and watched the clock.

It was the longest day of his life. He hadn't wanted to go to school. He wanted to chase his dog...or whatever his dog had turned into. But his mother had made him go to school. She didn't want to hear about monsters in the backyard. All she knew was that they had been robbed. Still, life had to go on.

But how could life go on, Hank wondered, if his beloved Montana had morphed into a monster?

Finally, three o' clock arrived. The bell rang. Hank was up and out the door.

He ran all the way home. When he reached the back gate, he stopped.

After waiting for this moment all day, now he was scared. Trembling, he pushed the gate open.

Everything was torn apart. Piles of dirt towered over him. Where the backyard had once been, there was now an enormous hole.

The only tree still standing was the old oak in the far corner of the yard. Its roots were exposed, but it stood like an island in a stormy sea of earth.

Hank stumbled across the ruined yard toward the giant oak. He grasped a branch and leaned over the pit. Clouds of steam rose into his face.

He heard a growl, then a hideous roar. Hank jumped back and wrapped his arms around the tree trunk.

Then he heard
something else: a dry,
rustling voice, whispering.

The boy looked around
the yard. There was no
one there.

He heard the whispering
again. It came from the tree!
From inside the oak!

Hank pressed his ear
to the bark. He heard
words now.

"The dragon…" it said.

"The dragon?" Hank asked.

Loud and clear now, the dry voice said,
"The dragon has woken!"

6

"Come nearer," the voice from the tree said.

"I'm as close as I can get," Hank said. He was hugging the tree. "Who are you? *What* are you?"

"I am Magnus the Last," the tree explained. "I am the last of the great Druid wizards."

"What are you doing…inside a tree?" Hank asked.

"I am under a spell, cast by the foulest creature the earth has ever known, the vile dragon Vanquar! The one who has woken!"

"Woken?" Hank exclaimed. "What do you mean?"

"Dragon magic, boy!" the voice said. "The dragon magic lives on in the bones!"

"You mean that was a *dragon* bone Montana ate yesterday?" Hank's knees started to give out. He gripped the tree even harder.

"Indeed it was," the wizard said.

"So that's why Montana turned into a monster?" Hank asked.

"The dragon is using the dog's life force to live again."

"What was a dragon bone doing in my backyard?"

"I killed the beast!" cried the wizard. "Eight hundred years ago, on this very spot, we battled to the death."

"But..." Hank began.

"Listen! We fought for three days and

nights. Then I summoned all my magic for one last spell. I blasted the dragon."

"But..."

"As he died, he threw a powerful curse upon me." The wizard's voice began to shake. "In a burst of flame, he caused my staff to grow large. It turned into a tree. Suddenly, I was sucked inside! The tree became my prison! Here I have remained, trapped, for eight hundred years!"

"That's awful," Hank whispered.

"I was awake, but, after so long a time, I had almost forgotten how to speak. Now the dragon lives again, and I have returned to my senses. He will destroy everything! Only you can stop him!"

"*M-me?*" Hank stammered.

"You and I together will stop him by destroying him and burning his bones! I will teach you magic."

Suddenly, a roaring wind blasted up from the depths of the pit. Hank clung to the tree.

"Vanquar the Vile!" Magnus cried out. "You must slay the beast!"

"I won't kill my dog!"

"Cinders and ashes, boy! Do *you* want to die?"

"I'm not killing my dog!" Hank said, setting his jaw.

"Act now!" the wizard urged. "Take my staff."

"What staff?"

The branch above Hank moved. Not like a branch in a breeze. More like a snake. *Writhing!*

"Take it!" the wizard commanded.

Hank grabbed the branch and pulled.

It stretched like bubble gum and snapped free.

A surge of power shot up Hank's arm.

The wizard said, "That's better. Now I can move about."

"Are you in *here* now?" Hank asked, staring at the staff.

"I am," Magnus said. "In your hand you hold more power than you have ever known. You must do exactly as I say."

"Will I kill Montana if I kill the dragon?" Hank asked. His stomach felt as if it was filled with hot mud.

"Spiders and flies! Be brave, boy!"

"Montana's my best friend!" Hank cried. "I won't kill him! You've been stuck in a tree for a jillion years. You don't *have* any best friends. Why should I listen to you, anyway? You're just a stick!"

The staff flickered. A jolt shot up Hank's arm.

"*Yow!*" Hank screamed.

"That's for talking back," the wizard scolded.

"Do that again," Hank warned, "and you're firewood!"

"Will you slay the dragon?" the wizard demanded.

Hank held the staff tightly. "I'm going to save my dog," he said.

He marched to the edge of the pit and looked down, his heart beating wildly.

7

Hank sat down at the edge of the hole. His legs squished in the mud.

The sides of the pit were steep. Hank took a deep breath, then slid down.

Caked with mud, he reached the bottom. It was dark down here!

"When we come upon the creature, keep your gaze fixed upon him," the wizard said through the staff. "Whatever you do, *don't* look at his treasure! If you look at it, you will fall under the dragon's spell! A dragon's treasure gives him power. It makes his magic stronger. It is what makes the dragon immortal."

Then Magnus said, "Now, boy—we'll start with the simplest spell."

Hank gripped the staff tighter and said, "Okay."

"Make light," Magnus commanded. "Think of nothing but the staff. Feel nothing but the staff. Are you doing it?"

"Yes," Hank replied.

"Now, imagine it glowing, and say these words." The wizard whispered them.

Hank repeated, *"Magnus lux!"*

"Now," Magnus urged, "stamp the staff on the ground!"

Hank did. The staff's tip glowed blue. It lit up the dark pit.

"Splendid!" Magnus said. "Now we can see where we're going."

Hank could see where he was going, all

right. But he wasn't sure he wanted to go there!

A tunnel stretched before him. Huge clawed footprints marked the slimy mud.

Hank clenched his teeth and started walking. As he moved farther into the tunnel, it grew hotter. Steam rose around him. The staff-light flickered.

The air smelled skunky—like Montana's foul breath last night.

Hank heard wheezing and belching up ahead. He stopped.

"Dim the light," the wizard urged. "Stamp the staff upon the ground! Quickly!"

Hank stamped the staff. The light dimmed. Then he saw a red glow up ahead.

"It's the beast!" Magnus whispered. "Probably feasting on some young princess."

"Montana wouldn't eat anybody!" Hank said.

"What's that I hear?" a rumbling voice called out.

Hank shivered.

"Answer me!" the dragon roared. "I can smell you!" Then he murmured, "Come to me. I have toys. Come see!"

"Boy," Magnus called from the staff, "are you prepared for battle?"

8

"I hear you tiptoeing," the dragon said. "Are you a little fairy? Are you an elf?"

Hank tightened his grip on the staff and swallowed hard.

Thick vapor swirled around the dragon.

His scales were green and shiny. Steam rose from his nostrils. Jagged horns jutted out from his forehead.

His fangs reached far below his jaws.

Hank looked into his eyes.

They were red, glowing snake eyes. Like the ones Hank had seen yesterday in his bedroom, burning in Montana's head!

The creature rested on a pile of rotting dragon bones. They were the bones of his ancient body—before he got hold of Montana's body and turned it into a hideous monster!

Hank heard a rattling and tinkling. A glimmer caught his eye.

Something lay nestled between the dragon's forelegs. It was dazzling. Sparkling and brilliant. Hank stared, fascinated.

Magnus shouted, "Boy, do not look at the treasure!"

But Hank couldn't help it. "Are you crazy?" he said. "It's just my mom's silverware. It can't hurt me!"

The staff flashed. A painful jolt shot up Hank's arm.

"*Ow!*" he cried. He snapped out of it.

"Remember what I told you, boy!"

Magnus warned. "*All* dragon treasure is dangerous! Don't look at it!"

"Look at them," the dragon purred, playing with his trinkets. "Look at my pretties...!"

Hank couldn't help himself. He looked and saw something twirling on the end of one of Vanquar's claws. *His dad's watch!* Now he knew he had to get the treasure back.

Tearing his gaze away from the watch, the boy stared into Vanquar's eyes. *Montana's in there*, he thought. *Somehow, I've got to get him back!*

"Now the battle begins," Magnus said.

Vanquar shifted on his pile of bones. "What's this?" he said, sniffing. "I smell wizard!" He roared and slammed his tail onto the ground.

"It's you!" Vanquar howled. He reared up and glared at the staff in Hank's grasp. "How did you escape, wizard?"

Hank hid the staff behind his back.

"Hiding behind a boy, are you?" Vanquar taunted. "Using him to fight your battles? Well, I've got a quick way to get rid of him! Fun for me, bad for the boy."

The creature raised himself up even taller. Huge black bat wings spread out behind him.

"Make a shield!" Magnus shouted. "Hold the staff before you and shout, *'Magnus protectica!'*"

"*Magnus protectica!*" Hank heard himself shouting as he imagined a shield.

"Now twirl the staff about!"

Hank spun the oak branch before him like a baton. It whirled into a shield of bright blue light. Vanquar blasted flame at Hank.

The force of the fireball threw the boy against the wall. But the shield saved him from being broiled alive.

"I'll get you later, you wretched slime!" Vanquar shrieked. "I've more important things to do now!"

The dragon scooped up his treasure.

With a flap of his mighty wings, Vanquar whooshed away down the tunnel.

"After him!" Magnus shouted.

Hank ran.

"Wizard!" the dragon roared from up ahead. "You can't stop me, even with your boy helping. Because now—I *remember!*"

"No!" Magnus yelled.

"I'm going there now," the dragon jeered. "You'll never stop me again!"

There came a noise like a hundred jet engines revving all at once. The dragon shot up out of the tunnel.

"He remembers his treasure!" Magnus screamed over the din.

"His treasure?" Hank asked. "His treasure's here."

"That's nothing! That's just something to tide him over."

"I don't get it," Hank said.

"You see, I could kill him before only by luring him away from his gold. If the dragon gets to his *real* treasure, then his power will increase. He will be unbeatable! Go!"

Hank ran back through the tunnel toward daylight. He climbed up out of the slimy pit.

Vanquar was in the yard, stretching his mighty wings. He flapped them and leaped upward. The air whirled around Hank. Dirt filled his eyes, stinging.

"Go! Go!" the wizard shouted.

Hank tore past the piles of earth and through the gate.

"Snails and turtles! Go after him!" Magnus yelled.

"I'm running as fast as I can."

"Larks and sparrows, boy! You can *fly!*"

"I can?" Hank asked.

"Of course you can. A simple magic spell. But we must hurry! Think of yourself flying."

"Okay," Hank said. He imagined the staff lifting him up.

"Now say these words as loudly as you can: *'Magnus levitatus!'*"

Hank screamed, *"Magnus levi...levi..."*

" '*...lev-i-TA-tus!*' " Magnus yelled.

"*...lev-i-TA-tus!*" Hank screamed as his feet left the ground. "Whoaaaa!"

9

Wind rushed past Hank's face. It roared in his ears. He looked down at the streets and houses below. He felt dizzy and excited.

Up ahead, the dragon circled and paused. He circled again, peering down.

"He doesn't know where he is!" Magnus shouted. "The land has changed in eight hundred years. This gives us time! Faster! Higher! Catch up with the fiend. Blast him out of the skies!"

Hank imagined going faster, and he sped up. His left hand slipped off the staff. He dangled by one hand as he flew.

"Hold on!" Magnus cried. "You can't stop the dragon if you're a heap of broken bones!"

Suddenly, the dragon folded his wings and dived.

"He's heading for the mall!" Hank yelled.

Crossroads Mall lay below them. Its parking lot was packed with cars. People milled about. They heard the *whoosh* as the dragon swooped above them.

Looking up, they saw the monster. They ran, screaming, and bumped into each other. Car tires screeched and horns beeped. A van plowed into a station wagon. A delivery truck smashed through the window of a music store.

Vanquar blew fire at the mall roof.

"Oh, no!" Hank cried. "My mom's in there!" His hands grew sweaty. *He'd already lost his dad. Was his mom going to die, too?* "Magnus!

Mom works in the mall! We've got to save her!"

Again, Vanquar blasted the roof like a giant blowtorch. The heat singed Hank's face. His sweaty hand slipped off the staff!

He fell, screaming, and landed in a Dumpster. The staff bonked him on the head.

"Worms and apples!" Magnus said. "At

least you didn't have far to fall!"

Hank crawled out of the stinking bin. He saw the dragon clawing at the now-blazing roof of the mall. Flaming chunks of roof sailed down onto the parking lot.

Then Vanquar disappeared inside.

"He's inside the mall!" Hank cried.

He pushed through the stampeding crowd,

dodging people and baby strollers.

A man screamed, "It's the end of the world!"

Hank finally reached the glass doors. He shoved them open and found himself on the mall's upper level. He looked around, but saw nothing but black smoke.

Coughing, Hank felt his way farther into the building.

The gallery railing loomed ahead. Black smoke billowed up, out the hole in the ceiling, and into the blue sky above.

He heard scraping in the courtyard below. He peered down over the railing. He could just make out the shape of the dragon. Vanquar was digging in the mall fountain.

"Stop!" Hank yelled, but Vanquar paid no attention. Then he tried a stern "Montana! No!"

The dragon paused and looked up.

Vanquar clawed the air with his forepaws, then slammed them down and dug more furiously than ever.

"Blast him!" Magnus bellowed. "Now, while he's digging! Blast him!"

"Blast him?" Hank cried. "How?"

"Raise the staff!"

Hank raised the staff.

"Take aim," the wizard instructed, "and say these words: *'Magnus obliteratus!'*"

But before Hank could aim, the dragon dropped out of sight through the hole he'd dug in the fountain!

"Toadstools and mushrooms, lad!" Magnus exclaimed. "You'll have to be faster than that if you're going to get out of this alive. Now we shall have to go down after him! Down into the monster's lair!"

"That's bad, huh?" Hank asked.

"You have no idea how bad. Take us down

to the fountain," the wizard commanded.

Hank used the spell Magnus had taught him. He floated over the gallery railing and down to the mall's lower level.

Gently, he landed in the ruined fountain. The dragon had burrowed a tunnel beneath it. Water gushed down the dark hole.

"Be quick, boy!" Magnus urged. "No time to lose!"

Hank hesitated. "Shouldn't we check on Mom first?" he said.

"There will be nothing and no one to save if we let the monster reach his treasure! Go!"

Hank looked down the hole into pitch blackness.

He gripped the staff tightly, took a deep breath, and said, *"Magnus levitatus!"*

Slowly he descended down, down, into darkness.

"Quickly, boy!" Magnus urged him.

Hank spoke through gritted teeth. "I've had just about enough of your nagging. My back hurts. My head hurts. I'm worried about my dog. I'm worried about my mom. Why can't you just lay off!"

The tunnel seemed to go down forever. It got darker and darker. Hank slowed down.

"Merlin's breath, boy, don't stop now!"

Hank hit the ground and slipped. He landed in a heap. The staff went spinning from his hand.

"No!" the boy screamed in the darkness. He groped along the slimy floor. Where was the staff?

Please, please, please, Hank thought, *please let me find Magnus. Don't make me do this alone.*

"Magnus!" he called out. "Where are you? I take back everything I said! You can talk as much as you want! Just help me find you! Please, please, please, Magnus!"

He groped desperately. Finally, his hand bumped something. The staff!

"Yes!" Hank cried. "Thank you!"

He grabbed it.

"…and bats, boy! Are you blind?"

"What?" Hank asked. "I dropped the staff. I couldn't hear you."

"Never mind. Give us light!" Magnus said.

Hank shouted, *"Magnus lux!"* and stamped the staff on the ground.

The tip of the staff shimmered with blue light. Hank gasped at what he saw. The caves seemed to go on forever!

Cones of hardened ooze hung from the ceiling. The floor was pitted and cracked.

"You are standing in the original lair," Magnus said quietly. "The beast built it over the centuries. One could get lost in here and never see daylight again."

Hank wrinkled his nose. "It stinks!"

"Breathe through your mouth," the wizard instructed.

Hank tried it. "Great. Now it *tastes* stinky!"

Hank crept deeper into the tunnel. It was getting hotter. He heard the *drip, drip* of water. His feet crunched on hardened slime.

"Hedgehogs and rabbits! Are you awake? The dragon escapes deeper into his lair! Can't you *sense* him? Move!"

Hank began to run. Magnus shouted directions: "Left! Now right! Another left!"

Each step led Hank deeper into the caves, toward the heat. Now it scorched his cheeks. It even chapped his lips.

Rounding a bend, he bumped into something hard. And leathery. And stinky. And hot.

He staggered backward in horror.

10

"Arrrrghhhh!" the dragon howled.

The shock wave blasted Hank backward.

"*Magnus frigidus!*" the wizard shouted. "Say it!"

The boy opened his mouth and screamed: "*Magnus frigidus!*"

A blast of shimmering frost shot from the staff.

Vanquar spat flame.

Ice and fire met! With a thunderclap, they canceled each other out.

Vanquar let out a frustrated screech. He

spun around and dug at a pile of rubble blocking his way.

"Pebbles and stones, lad!" Magnus shouted. "The worm is trapped! Blast him!"

But Vanquar broke through the wall of rocks and vanished into the darkness.

"Ticks and tocks!" cried the wizard. "You're too slow!"

Hank climbed over the rubble. He stopped.

A vast cavern yawned before him. At its center, the dragon crouched atop a small, shimmering mountain of gems and coins. There were swords, armor, and crowns of gold and silver.

Standing or lying, here and there, were a dozen or so life-size statues. There were statues of warriors with swords and shields. Statues of dwarfs raising battle-axes above their heads. Statues of princesses in flowing gowns, their mouths open, silently screaming.

The statues looked eerily lifelike. And, on closer inspection, they seemed to be made of gold! Solid gold! Glittering.

Inviting Hank to touch them.

Never had he seen such riches!

And then he knew exactly what he was going to do.

He would steal the dragon's treasure! Just *one* of those statues would make him rich!

He moved toward the glittering mound, reaching out a trembling hand. All he wanted in this world was to touch the dragon's treasure.

11

The dragon chuckled. Idly, he slid golden rings onto his sharp talons. He draped a pearl necklace around his neck.

"What did I tell you?" Vanquar purred to Hank. "Aren't they pretty? Have some, my little warrior. Share my treasure."

Vanquar dangled a diamond necklace before the boy. "Come," he coaxed. "Come and touch."

Magnus's voice boomed forth like thunder: *"Do not fall under the spell of the treasure! Don't look at it!"*

The wizard sent a stinging jolt through Hank. But this time Hank shrugged it off.

He felt only a burning need to touch the treasure.

Magnus shouted, "The spell has got you!" Then he boomed once again: *"Boy! Look at your feet!"*

Hank barely heard the wizard. But something weird was happening to his feet. He looked down.

He tried to wiggle his toes. His feet were numb. His sneakers and the bottoms of his jeans had turned to gold! But he didn't care. Actually, he kind of liked it.

His only thought was: *Gold!*

"Don't you see?" Magnus screamed at him. "*This* is what happens when you fall under the spell of the treasure! *You* turn into gold!"

Hank was thinking: *I'll be rich.*

"Look at you!" Magnus went on. "Do you

not see the statues everywhere? These lifeless things are his victims. Once you turn into gold, all is lost!"

Hank looked at his feet. He watched, fascinated, as the gold slowly crept up his legs.

Magnus yelled, "Destroy the dragon! Now!"

Destroy him? Hank almost laughed. He wanted to *thank* him! Imagine— turning him into gold. What could be better?

Then a curious thing happened. The dragon started to play in the piles of treasure.

He was whimpering. A very doglike whimper. He wagged his enormous tail, knocking over a statue.

He romped in the piles of jewelry and gold. Exactly the way Montana used to romp through mounds of autumn leaves.

Recognition flashed in Hank. It was just a flicker. But it was enough!

"Montana," he whispered.

"Good!" Magnus screamed. "Now listen. Brace yourself. I'm gathering all my power. Point the staff at the dragon!"

"But—Montana!" Hank protested.

"Do as I say!" the wizard screamed.

The dragon roared, "You can't hurt me now!"

Hank aimed the staff and shouted, *"Magnus obliteratus!"*

It fired with a deafening blast. Hank fell backward, stunned.

12

The smoke cleared. The dust settled. The dragon crouched before Hank. His eyes were filled with terrible pain and sadness.

Hank leaped up. Feeling had returned to his legs and feet. They were normal again.

The cavern floor was bare. The treasure was gone. Every last gem, gone. Every statue, every crown.

The dragon croaked, "What have you done?"

Hank found his voice. "I guess I trashed your treasure," he said.

"Noooooo!" the dragon wailed.

"You're powerless without it," Hank said.

Then he pleaded, "Magnus, I want my dog back! Please? Change Montana back!"

There was no answer. Hank looked at the staff in his hand. A smoking, blackened stump was all that remained.

Hank dropped it and looked around helplessly. "Magnus?" he called.

The dragon sniffed the ground. "My pretties," he moaned. "Gone!"

The creature clawed at his stomach. "All my pretties! Forever gone!"

He scratched faster, clawing his stomach and chest. As he did so, green scales fell.

The dragon scratched faster. More scales dropped. A shower of them. Vanquar howled.

Hank watched in horror as the dragon shredded himself into pieces. A leg here, a wing there. His ears and snout fell to the cavern floor.

The creature screeched and thrashed. Scales and teeth flew everywhere.

As the dragon fell apart, the light in the cavern faded.

Finally, there was no dragon-glow. No staff-light. Only darkness.

Hank was alone in the dark. No more dragon. No more Magnus. No more dog. Only himself and the sound of his own raspy breathing.

Then he heard another noise.

Weak at first, then stronger.

A familiar sound. A definitely doggy sound. Then he felt a warm, slobbery tongue on his cheek.

"Montana!" Hank shouted with joy.

13

"You're back!" Hank cried. He hugged his dog.

Montana yipped happily.

"Are you done being a dragon?" Hank clung to Montana's neck, loving the feel of the dog's fur beneath his hands. "I really missed you, mutt. But...we've got to get out of here and find Mom!"

The dog seemed to understand. He took Hank's hand gently in his jaws and tugged.

"You know the way, Montana?" Hank stumbled after the dog in the darkness.

Montana led him through one dark tunnel after another. Then Hank noticed two things: the ground sloped upward, and it was getting lighter.

They moved faster now, climbing. He could actually see Montana at his side.

His feet hit on concrete. The walls, too, were concrete. Before them yawned the narrow opening of a storm drain!

Hank and Montana crawled out. It was night. They weren't at the mall. They were several streets away, and only a few blocks from home!

"Good job, boy! Let's get home. Maybe Mom's there!"

But when they got to the house, it was dark and empty. Montana raced to the back gate and pushed it open.

"Montana! Come back!" Hank panicked.

He ran after his dog, screaming, "Don't eat any bones!"

When Hank reached the gate, he stopped. The yard was back to normal! The mounds of earth were gone! There was no gaping hole. No mess.

Stranger still, the oak tree was gone!

A man stood in its place.

He grasped a wooden staff. It glowed brightly.

He looked like a gnome in a tattered robe. Oak leaves clung to his hat.

Hank stared. The old man picked an acorn out of his long, mossy green beard.

Montana went up to the stranger and sat calmly at his feet.

"Magnus?" Hank asked. "Is that you?"

"Knots and splinters, boy! Who else?"

"You're *alive!*" Hank yelped. "And so is my dog!"

Magnus smiled. His eyes twinkled. "The spell is broken! How did you do it?"

"I couldn't kill my dog," Hank explained to the wizard. "So I blasted the treasure

instead. You told me it gave Vanquar his power."

"Incredible!" the wizard exclaimed. "Why didn't *I* think of that?"

"Have you seen my mom?" Hank asked.

"I haven't seen anything but my feet. Warts and bunions! It feels good to wiggle my toes again!"

Hank bit his lip. Tears came to his eyes. "But my mom was in the mall…"

"Brooms and dustbins, lad! You haven't said a word about the yard! I cleaned it up!"

"Uh. Yeah. Thanks," Hank said dully.

"The least I could do. But first I destroyed the dragon bones! Can't have that happening all over again, can we?" He chuckled.

"But my mom…"

"Your mother is safe," Magnus said gently. "No need to worry!"

"How do you know?" Hank asked.

"Magic of the staff, boy! I'm a wizard."

"Well, where *is* she?"

"On her way here."

"Great!" Hank felt a surge of relief.

But then it hit him. He and his mom were right back where they started. No treasure. No money. No hope. He slumped to the ground.

Then he got an idea. "I was wondering..." he began.

"Wondering?" the wizard prodded.

"If dragon magic lives forever, and if *you* can come back to life after being a tree... I wondered..."

"Get to the point, boy, before I start growing roots again!"

"Could you...uhm...bring my dad back to life?"

The wizard sighed and gazed up at the starry sky. "I wish I could, my boy. But the truth is...there are some things that even magic cannot change."

"Oh," Hank said sadly.

Magnus rested a gentle hand on Hank's shoulder. "But know this, my boy," he said softly. "Your father and the angels celebrate your bravery this day.

"As for treasure," Magnus went on, "perhaps not all is lost." He slapped Hank on the back. Then he reached into his robe and dangled something before Hank.

"This is for you, my boy."

The wizard held something shiny. Something gold. Hank took it.

"A watch!" Hank said.

"Not just *any* watch," the wizard said.

"My *dad's* watch!" Hank said softly.

14

"I think you've earned it, my boy."

"Terrific!" Hank said. "Thanks!"

"You're welcome, my boy."

"How did you get it?" Hank asked. "Did you use magic? This solves everything! You can just whip up some gold or something! Mom will never have to work again!"

"Whip up some gold?" Magnus cried. "Bricks and bats! Have you learned nothing?"

The wizard rapped Hank on the head with his staff. "Dragon magic is the only power that turns anything into gold. And even that will only work on living creatures—as you yourself should know.

"If everyone could make gold, it would be worthless. If just anyone could do it, every sorcerer's apprentice would be driving a golden chariot! I did *not* 'just whip up' your father's watch. I *found* it in the yard when I tidied up. As simple and as ordinary as that!"

"Oh," Hank whispered.

"Pennies and peacocks!" Magnus roared. "Where's your spirit? You've just defeated an evil monster! Don't give up now! Since you're my apprentice, I expect you to live life with gusto!"

"What?" Hank asked.

"I said I was Magnus the Last, the last of the great Druid wizards. But no more. I have found someone to take up my staff! You, my boy!"

"I'm your *apprentice?*" Hank sputtered.

"And," Magnus continued, "I seem to recall that wizards and their apprentices made a pretty good living in my day. We just might be able to help out your dear mother."

"Hey, that's not a bad idea!" Hank agreed. "Street musicians and jugglers make good money down on Pearl Street. Maybe we can, too!"

Magnus frowned. "I'd like to think we'll do more than perform tricks for a few pennies. Real magic is serious business!"

"Excellent!" Hank cried. "You mean it? I can work with you?"

"Shouts and echoes! Weren't you listening? Of course! You'll make a fine wizard!"

Magnus tilted his head, listening. "Your dear mother approaches," he said.

Sure enough, the old Chevy rattled to a stop out front. Hank jumped up and ran into the house. Montana trailed behind him.

His mother slammed the front door. She saw her son and cried, *"Hank!"*

"Mom!" Hank shouted. He ran to hug her.

"You're okay!" she sobbed. "I...have... been...so...scared! But you're okay!"

She hugged him tightly again. "There was this terrible fire. The mall burned to the ground! Oh, Hank," she said.

"Mom," Hank said, "it's okay now. Believe me. We'll be fine. And look!" He dangled his father's watch.

"Oh, Hank," she said. Her face brightened into a smile. "You found it!"

Montana came up and nuzzled Hank's hand. The boy hugged his dog.

"And Montana's back!" she exclaimed.

"He sure is!"

Absently patting the dog, she said, "The shop burned down. I'm out of a job. It'll take a miracle to get our lives back together."

"A miracle?" Hank said. "Funny you should say that." He walked to the kitchen window and looked out.

There was Magnus, leaning on his staff, still standing where the old oak used to be. He was looking up at the stars. The wind wafted through his mossy hair and stirred his robe.

"Mom," Hank called, "come here. There's somebody I want you to meet. Then we can all go out for ice cream to celebrate."

His mom looked at him blankly. "Celebrate?" she asked in a tired voice. "Oh, Hank, I don't think I feel up to meeting any-one...or driving."

"Larks and sparrows, Mom!" Hank exclaimed. "Who said anything about *driving?* We're gonna *fly!*"

About the Authors

PAUL HINDMAN lives in Boulder, Colorado, with his son, Jesse (also a writer), and his four-year-old daughter, Dakota (who can write her name without any help). Paul teaches English and writes short stories and novels. In his spare time, he works forty hours a week for the University of Colorado.

NATE EVANS lives and works in Kansas City, Missouri. He gets most of his ideas while sleeping. One night he had a dream about a boy watching a dog flying with a big bone in its mouth. From this weird little image, Paul and Nate created *Dragon Bones.*

Nate is currently trying to learn telepathy so that when he writes with Paul, they won't need to use the phone. This will save big on phone bills, and then Nate can use that money to buy candy. Or maybe he'll get a dog.